SUMMER CAMP
SCIENCE
MYSTERIES

# #2 The Nighttime Cabin Thief

## A Mystery about Light

by Lynda Beauregard

illustrated by Der-shing Helmer

GRAPHIC UNIVERSE™ • MINNEAPOLIS • NEW YORK

Angie Rayez

Alex Rayez

Jordan Collins

Braelin Walker

Rashawn Walker

Carly Livingston

DON'T MISS THE EXPERIMENTS ON PAGES 44 AND 45!

MYSTERIOUS WORDS AND MORE ON PAGES 46 AND 47!

Kyle Reed

Loraine Sanders

# Light is a form of energy.

Light travels in waves and moves in straight lines. When light hits an object, the density (compactness) and color of the object determine whether the light bends, bounces off the object, is absorbed by the object, or passes right through it. When light passes through a lens, it can make objects look bigger or smaller than they really are.

Light bounces (reflects) off shiny surfaces such as mirrors. When you look in a mirror, you are seeing the light wave being reflected back exactly as it hit the mirror. Dull, dark objects absorb light rather than reflecting it back. Some substances, including water, bend light waves as the light passes through them.

Story by Lynda Beauregard
Illustrations by Der-shing Helmer
Coloring by Jenn Manley Lee
Lettering by Marshall Dillon

Graphic Universe™
A division of Lerner Publishing Group, Inc.
241 First Avenue North
Minneapolis, MN 55401 U.S.A.

Website address: www.lernerbooks.com

Main body text set in CCWildwords.
Typeface provided by Comicraft/Active Images.

Library of Congress Cataloging-in-Publication Data

Beauregard, Lynda.
        The nighttime cabin thief : a mystery about light / by Lynda Beauregard ;
    illustrated by Der-shing Helmer.
            p.   cm. — (Summer camp science mysteries)
        Summary: When several campers at Camp Dakota report missing items and
    begin pointing fingers at a fellow camper, a group of children search for the culprit.
    Includes glossary and experiments.
        ISBN: 978–0–7613–5692–9 (lib. bdg. : alk. paper)
        ISBN: 978–0–7613–8747–3 (eBook)
        1. Graphic novels.  [1. Graphic novels.  2. Camps—Fiction.  3. Light—Fiction.]
    I. Helmer, Der-shing, ill.  II. Title.
    PZ7.7.B42Ni  2012
    741.5'973—dc23                                          2011016593

Manufactured in the United States of America
2 –PP – 4/1/13

GIVE IT BACK.

GIVE **WHAT** BACK?

MY HORSEMANSHIP MEDAL! I KNOW YOU HAVE IT!

I DON'T EVEN KNOW WHAT THAT IS!

IT'S AN AWARD SHE GOT AT A RIDING COMPETITION.

SHE POLISHES IT EVERY NIGHT, THEN HANGS IT ON HER HEADBOARD.

HEY! THAT'S SECRET ROOMMATE STUFF!

ANYWAY, WHEN I WOKE UP THIS MORNING, IT WAS GONE.

MAYBE IT FELL ON THE FLOOR?

DID YOU FORGET TO HANG IT UP? IT MIGHT BE IN YOUR BED.

ALREADY LOOKED THERE.

I LOOKED THERE TOO.

HE TOOK IT!

HANG ON, CARLY. WHAT MAKES YOU THINK BRAELIN TOOK IT?

COME ON! HE'S **ALWAYS** GETTING INTO TROUBLE.

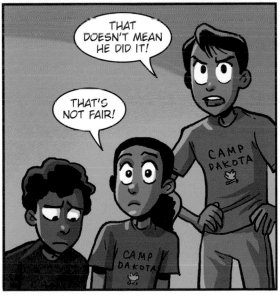

THAT DOESN'T MEAN HE DID IT!

THAT'S NOT FAIR!

HE'S NOT VERY SMART, EITHER. HE'S WEARING A DARK SHIRT ON A HOT, SUNNY DAY.

**EVERYONE** KNOWS YOU STAY COOLER IF YOU WEAR LIGHTER COLORS ON SUNNY DAYS.

WHITE CLOTHES REFLECT LIGHT. BLACK CLOTHES ABSORB IT.

Light turns into heat when it strikes objects. Because white objects reflect light, very little light becomes heat after hitting the objects. Black objects absorb light instead of reflecting it, so they also absorb more heat.

OKAY, BUT WHAT DOES THAT HAVE TO DO WITH BRAELIN AND YOUR MEDAL?

NEVER MIND!

ALL RIGHT, EVERYONE!

LET'S HEAD OVER TO THE ART CABIN!

GOOD QUESTION, ALEX! LIGHT COMES IN THROUGH THE TOP HOLE, BOUNCING OFF ONE MIRROR TOWARD THE OTHER ONE. THEN IT BOUNCES OFF THAT ONE TOWARD YOUR EYE, MOVING THROUGH THE BOTTOM HOLE.

When light hits a shiny surface, like a mirror, the light reflects off the surface in the same pattern as when it made contact. Dull surfaces will scatter light in all directions when it bounces off them.

OKAY, BUT WE DON'T WANT TO SEE JUST LIGHT.

WE WANT TO SEE PEOPLE AND TREES AND STUFF.

IMAGES ARE MADE OF LIGHT.

OUR EYES AND BRAINS TAKE THAT LIGHT AND MAKE IT INTO SOMETHING WE CAN RECOGNIZE.

THE FIRST MIRROR IN A PERISCOPE INVERTS AN IMAGE. THE SECOND MIRROR INVERTS IT AGAIN, SO IT APPEARS NORMAL WHEN IT REACHES US.

COOL!

OKAY, EVERYONE. IF YOU'RE DONE, LET'S PUT EVERYTHING AWAY SO WE CAN GO PLAY ON THE BEACH!

THIS IS THE STORY FROM THE DAKOTA SIOUX NATIVE AMERICANS...

ONCE THERE WAS A YOUNG SIOUX BOY NAMED KOSUMI.

HE CAUGHT FOOD FOR HIS FAMILY BY HUNTING, BUT HE WASN'T VERY GOOD AT FISHING. AND KOSUMI REALLY LIKED TO EAT FISH.

ONE DAY, A HAWK NAMED CHATAN BEGAN TO WATCH KOSUMI AS HE TRIED TO FISH.

CHATAN LAUGHED EVERY TIME HE MISSED.

WHY ARE YOU LAUGHING AT ME?

CATCHING FISH WITH A SPEAR IS HARD!

INDEED, IT IS VERY HARD... WHEN YOU DO IT WRONG!

WHAT DOES A BIRD KNOW ABOUT FISHING?

HOW DID YOU DO THAT?

IT IS EASY, ONCE YOU KNOW THE TRICK.

THE SALMON TRY TO FOOL YOU. IN THE WATER, THE FISH LOOK AS IF THEY ARE IN ONE SPOT. BUT WHEN YOU TRY TO CATCH THEM, THEY ARE NOT THERE.

HOW CAN THEY NOT BE WHERE I SEE THEM? WHEN I THROW MY SPEAR AT A DEER, I NEVER MISS.

THE WATER PROTECTS THE SALMON. IT MAKES IT SEEM AS IF THE SALMON ARE BIGGER, AND CLOSER TO THE SURFACE, THAN THEY REALLY ARE.

SO IF YOU AIM YOUR SPEAR LOWER AND FARTHER AWAY THAN YOUR EYES TELL YOU TO, YOU MAY CATCH YOUR DINNER AFTER ALL.

KOSUMI TRIED AGAIN, FOLLOWING THE HAWK'S ADVICE.

HE AIMED HIS SPEAR A LITTLE LOWER AND HE CAUGHT HIS FIRST SALMON!

AND CHATAN DECIDED THAT SALMON WAS A FINE REWARD FOR HIS ADVICE.

AND *THAT* IS HOW THE HAWK TAUGHT THE DAKOTA SIOUX HOW TO FISH.

BUT THE WATER ISN'T REALLY MAGIC, IS IT?

HOW DID IT HIDE THE SALMON?

IT'S NOT MAGIC-- IT'S REFRACTION!

HUH?

WATER BENDS LIGHT. THAT BENDING MAKES THE FISH LOOK CLOSER THAN IT IS.

Water is denser than air. When a wave of light enters water, it slows down. The change in speed also changes the light wave's direction, "bending" it. This makes underwater objects appear to be in a different location when viewed from above.

SO NOW THAT WE KNOW THE HAWK'S SECRET TO CATCHING FISH, WHO WANTS TO GIVE IT A TRY TOMORROW AFTERNOON?

THE NEXT MORNING

WELL, I CERTAINLY DIDN'T TAKE IT.

THEN WHO DID?

TOOK WHAT?

MY MONEY! GLORIA TRADED $1.50 FOR THE BEAD NECKLACE I MADE YESTERDAY, AND NOW ALL SIX QUARTERS ARE GONE!

GEE, I WONDER WHO COULD HAVE STOLEN THEM?

MAYBE . . .

HEY, WHERE'S BRAELIN?

WE HAVEN'T SEEN HIM. WHY?

BECAUSE I'M GOING TO PUNCH HIM, THAT'S WHY!

WHOA! HANG ON...

JORDAN, HITTING HIM WON'T FIX ANYTHING.

WHY ARE YOU SO MAD AT HIM?

HE TOOK MY STAR!

YOUR WHAT?

MY... SHERIFF'S STAR. OH, NEVER MIND.

I CHECKED THE WHOLE ROOM WHILE BRAELIN WAS AWAY. IT'S NOT THERE, JORDAN.

WHERE DID YOU LAST SEE IT?

ON THE TABLE NEAR MY BED.

MY MONEY WAS ON THE TABLE IN MY ROOM!

LOOKS LIKE BRAELIN WAS *PRETTY* BUSY LAST NIGHT.

WHY ARE ALL OF YOU SO SURE THAT BRAELIN TOOK YOUR STUFF?

WELL, HE *DID* DISAPPEAR LAST NIGHT. THE REST OF US WERE AT THE CAMPFIRE.

BRAELIN'S LOST SOMETHING TOO. MAYBE HE DIDN'T TAKE YOUR STAR.

OR MAYBE HE'S MAKING THIS UP SO WE WON'T YELL AT HIM.

I DIDN'T TAKE ANYTHING FROM ANYBODY!

BRAELIN, COME BACK!

BRAELIN--

NO! WHY DOESN'T ANYONE BELIEVE ME?

I'M GOING TO FOLLOW HIM. MAYBE I'LL FIND WHERE HE HID OUR STUFF.

SO? DID HE ADMIT IT?

NOPE.

COME ON. LET'S HEAD BACK TO OUR CABIN. I HAVE AN IDEA.

WHAT KIND OF CLUES ARE WE LOOKING FOR?

ANYTHING. FOOTPRINTS, SOMETHING HE MIGHT HAVE DROPPED . . .

AH! FINGERPRINTS!

WE NEED A MICROSCOPE. OR A MAGNIFYING GLASS.

SEE HERE?

ALL I CAN SEE IS A SMUDGE.

NO PROBLEM! I KNOW HOW TO MAKE ONE.

WE JUST NEED THIS PAPER CLIP, A PENCIL, AND A LITTLE BIT OF WATER.

THERE'S STILL SOME WATER LEFT IN THIS CUP.

PERFECT!

FIRST, WE MAKE THE FRAME.

AND THIS WATER WILL MAKE THE LENS.

HUH? HOW CAN WATER BE A LENS?

THE WATER STICKS TO THE EDGES OF THE PAPER CLIP, BUT IT HANGS DOWN IN THE MIDDLE, MAKING A BOWL SHAPE.

A lens refracts light. Refraction makes objects appear either bigger or smaller, depending on which way light curves and by how much.

IT ISN'T AS STRONG AS A REAL MICROSCOPE, BUT IT'LL MAGNIFY THESE FINGERPRINTS WELL ENOUGH FOR US TO SEE THEM.

COOL!

SEE? A CLUE!

BUT WHOSE FINGERPRINT IS IT?

HMM. I KNOW! YOU MAKE A FINGERPRINT RIGHT NEXT TO IT. WE'LL COMPARE THEM.

AHA! THEY'RE DIFFERENT. THE FIRST ONE MUST BE BRAELIN'S!

NO, THAT JUST MEANS THAT THE FIRST FINGERPRINT ISN'T MINE. IT COULD BE YOURS.

OH... RIGHT.

TRY TO MAKE A FINGERPRINT ON THE OTHER SIDE OF IT. WE'LL COMPARE THEM.

SEE? THEY'RE THE SAME.

IT WAS YOUR FINGERPRINT ALL ALONG.

OH.

I DON'T SEE ANYTHING ELSE THAT COULD BE A CLUE IN HERE.

LET'S LOOK AROUND OUTSIDE.

BRAELIN?

WHAT DID YOU TAKE NOW?

I DIDN'T TAKE ANYTHING! BUT I DID *FIND* SOMETHING.

SHOW ME.

THAT'S FROM MY MEDAL!

IT WAS ON THE GROUND OVER THERE.

I DON'T KNOW. MAYBE SOMEONE WAS DRAGGING IT?

BUT WHERE'S THE REST OF IT? HOW DID THE RIBBON GET TORN OFF?

THAT'S RIDICULOUS!

WHATCHA GOT THERE?

A CLUE.

LET'S LOOK AROUND FOR MORE!

I FOUND SOME YELLOW THREADS. LOOKS LIKE THEY MATCH.

WHOEVER TOOK IT MUST HAVE GONE THIS WAY.

LOOK! A QUARTER! I BET IT'S ONE OF MINE.

HMM. THE ONLY THING IN THAT DIRECTION IS . . .

THE ART CABIN!

WAIT! I DON'T THINK WE'RE ALLOWED TO GO IN THE ART CABIN WITHOUT A COUNSELOR.

ARTS & CRAFTS CABIN

ARE YOU SCARED?

WE'RE JUST GOING TO LOOK AROUND.

C'MON. I WANT TO FIND MY MONEY!

WE AREN'T GOING TO FIND ANYTHING HERE.

BRAELIN PROBABLY BURIED THE STUFF SOMEWHERE.

I *TOLD* YOU...

THUMP

THUMP THUMP

WHOA!

WHAT IS THAT?

LET'S GET OUT OF HERE!

WAS THAT A GHOST?

I THINK IT CAME FROM THE ATTIC.

MAYBE IT WAS THE THIEF!

I THOUGHT YOU SAID I WAS THE THIEF.

MAYBE IT'S YOUR PARTNER IN CRIME.

WE NEED TO GET UP THERE AND TAKE A LOOK.

I'M NOT GOING UP THERE!

NO WAY!

I HAVE A BETTER IDEA.

READY?

NOT REALLY.

PUSH!

CAN YOU SEE IT?

I CAN'T SEE ANYTHING. THERE'S NOT ENOUGH LIGHT.

WAIT...

YIKES! A MONSTER! RUN!

TWENTY MINUTES LATER

I'M PRETTY SURE IT WASN'T A MONSTER, BRAELIN.

BUT ITS EYES WERE HUGE, AND... EVIL-LOOKING.

I'M PRETTY SURE IT GROWLED AT US.

AN *EVIL* GROWL.

IT SOUNDS MORE LIKE A NOCTURNAL ANIMAL. MAYBE SOMETHING DECIDED TO SETTLE IN THAT ATTIC.

*HMM.* I'LL GO TAKE A LOOK.

CAN I COME TOO?

WHY WERE YOU KIDS POKING AROUND IN THE ART CABIN?

WE WERE LOOKING FOR OUR MISSING STUFF.

WHAT KIND OF STUFF?

WELL, I LOST A WATCH...

...AND THEN WE FOUND SOME CLUES THAT LED US HERE.

I SEE.

WELL, LET'S SEE WHAT'S UP HERE.

A-HA!

KYLE, LOOK BACK THERE!

KYLE'S BEEN GONE TOO LONG.

MAYBE THE MONSTER GOT HIM.

HE'LL BE FINE. HE HAS A MONSTER-HUNTING BADGE, YOU KNOW.

REALLY?

YOU GUYS! IT WAS A RACCOON!

NO WAY! THOSE EYES WERE *HUGE!*

NOCTURNAL ANIMALS HAVE BIG EYES. IT HELPS THEM SEE BETTER AT NIGHT.

THEIR EYES LET IN MORE LIGHT THAN OURS DO, SO THEY CAN SEE EVEN WHEN IT LOOKS PITCH-BLACK TO US.

I BET IT'S TOO BRIGHT FOR THEM TO SEE WELL DURING THE DAY.

SO *THAT'S* WHY THEY ONLY COME OUT AT NIGHT.

ALL RIGHT THEN.

C'MON, LORAINE. LET'S ROUND UP THE OTHER KIDS FOR LUNCH.

WAIT-- I THINK WE ALL HAVE SOMETHING TO SAY TO BRAELIN.

WE DO? OH, YEAH.

SORRY, BRAELIN.

I'M SO SORRY, BRAELIN. I SHOULD HAVE BELIEVED IN YOU.

YEAH, ME TOO.

I'M JUST SO USED TO... WELL, NEVER MIND.

CAN YOU FORGIVE US?

42

THE END

# Experiments

Try these fun experiments at home or in your classroom.
Make sure you have an adult help out.

## Periscope

You will need: 2 (1 quart) milk cartons; scissors; 2 small, square mirrors; a utility knife (very sharp—ask an adult to help you with this); and masking or duct tape

1) Cut the tops off the milk cartons. They should now be rectangular boxes.

2) Using the scissors, cut out a square on the front side of each carton, near the bottom.

3) Lay the cartons down so that the sides with the cutout square face to the right.

4) Ask an adult to cut a short diagonal line across each carton on the side that's facing up. He or she should start near the bottom on the right side, moving up to the left. The diagonal line should be the same length as your mirrors. This will be a slot to hold the mirror in place.

5) Slide the mirrors into the cut lines. Hold up each carton and look through the square hole. You should be able to see the ceiling.

6) Squeeze the top end of one carton so it can slide easily into the top end of the other carton. The square holes should be on opposite sides.

7) Tape the two cartons together.

## How does it work?

Mirrors reflect light. Once light comes into the square hole on the top of the periscope, the first mirror reflects the light down to the second mirror. The second mirror reflects the light through the bottom square hole, reversing—and correcting—the image. Since mirrors reflect light waves exactly as they receive them, the image you see coming out of the periscope at the bottom is the same as the image that enters through the top.

# Coin Illusion

You will need: a bowl, a coin, and a large cup of water

1) Place the coin in the middle of the bowl.

2) Step back from the bowl. Keep moving back until you can no longer see the coin.

3) Stay where you are. Have someone slowly pour water from the cup into the bowl.

4) The coin will magically reappear!

## How does it work?

Water refracts, or bends, light waves. Without water in the bowl, the coin is hidden by the edge of the bowl. When you add water, the light wave that carries the image of the coin becomes bent as it travels through the water. The light eventually bends enough that you can see the coin over the edge of the bowl.

# Mysterious Words

**density:** a measure of mass per unit of volume

**nocturnal:** something that occurs in the night or is most active at night

**periscope:** an optical instrument that uses reflective surfaces such as mirrors to allow the user to see things that are not in the direct line of sight

**reflection:** the bouncing of light from a shiny surface

**refraction:** the turning or bending of light, when it passes from one medium into another that has a different density